To Tom, Sarah,
Nigel, Sabrina and Kim
for their kind help
and advice

Mommy Laid an Egg!

or Where *Do* Babies Come From?
by Babette Cole

chronicle books · san francisco

"Well," said mom and dad.
"We think it's time we
told you...

...how babies are made!"

"OK," we said.

"Girl babies are made from sugar and spice
and everything nice," said mom.

"Boy babies are made from slugs and snails and puppy dogs' tails!" said dad.

"Some babies are delivered by dinosaurs."

"You can make them out of gingerbread!" said mom.

"Sometimes, you just find them under stones," said dad.

"You can grow them

"...rom seeds," said mom.

"Or just squeeze them out of tubes!"

"Mommy laid an egg," said dad.

"It exploded!

And you shot out!"

"Hee hee hee, ha ha ha, hoo hoo hoo, what a
bunch of nonsense!" we laughed.
"But you were right about the SEEDS,
the TUBE, and the EGG!"

"We'll teach you how babies are really made."

"Mommies do have eggs. They are inside their bodies."

"And daddies have seeds in seed pods outside their bodies."

This fits

"Daddies also have a tube.
The seeds come out of
the pods and through the tube."

in here

"The tube goes into the mommy's body through a hole. Then the seeds swim inside using their tails!"

"Here are some ways…

...mommies and daddies
fit together."

"The Baby gets bigger...

"The Mommy gets fatter...

"So now YOU know...

...and so does everyone else!"

First published in the United States in 1993 by Chronicle Books.
First published in Great Britain in 1993 by Jonathan Cape Ltd.

Library of Congress Cataloging-in-Publication Data
Cole, Babette.
Mommy laid an egg! / by Babette Cole.
p.   cm.
Summary: Two children explain to their parents, using their own
drawings, where babies come from.
ISBN 0-8118-0350-3 (hardcover)
ISBN 0-8118-1319-3 (paperback)
1. Sex instruction for children--Juvenile literature. [1. Sex
instruction for children. 2. Reproduction.] I. Title.
HQ53.C64 1993
649'.657--cc20   92-38306
                                                      CIP
                                                       AC

ISBN 0-8118-0350-3

Printed in Singapore.

10 9 8 7 6 5 4 3 2

Chronicle Books LLC
85 Second Street
San Francisco, California 94105

www.chroniclebooks.com/Kids